ALLAN DRUMMOND
LIBERTY!

Frances Foster Books • Farrar, Straus and Giroux • New York

Imagine this . . . New York City, October 28, 1886 . . .

A small boy stands at the foot of an enormous statue, his heart bursting with excitement, for today he has been given the most important job in the world . . .

Imagine the man who designed the Statue of Liberty looking down on New York Harbor from the crown of his magnificent creation. Below him, hundreds of ships are bobbing about, waiting for the first glimpse of his brilliant masterpiece *Liberty Enlightening the World*. Thousands of people have gathered to celebrate the dedication of Frédéric Auguste Bartholdi's colossal sculpture.

Schoolchildren all over France have helped raise the money for the huge metal figure—a gift from the people of France to honor America's ideals of Liberty and Freedom. In the United States, Joseph Pulitzer's popular newspaper, *The World*, has championed the idea of the statue, and persuaded thousands of American schoolchildren and adults to give money to help raise the monument to Liberty on an island in New York Harbor.

Now the day has arrived. The mayor of New York City has proclaimed a public holiday, and Broadway is bustling with people who have come to watch the big parade. In the harbor, immigrants are arriving by ship to begin new lives, and two hundred women, members of the New York Suffrage Association, are also afloat, protesting. How, they demand, could Liberty be represented as a woman when women in the United States and France cannot even vote?

Imagine: in the great crowd of men gathered on the island, there are only two females allowed near the statue—the wife and daughter of a French engineer.

All is confusion, noise, and excitement. Through the shriek of ships' whistles and the swirling rainclouds Mr. Bartholdi peers down . . .

All of these facts—the rain, the noise, the confusion, the harbor filled with celebration, the crowds, Mr. Bartholdi waiting way up high in the crown of the Statue of Liberty for a signal from a small boy—all of these facts are true; I found them in the history books.

But nobody seems to have remembered who that small boy was, or exactly what he did on the day Mr. Bartholdi's wonderful statue lit up the world. People say that his signal was lost, or that a cannon went off, or that Mr. Bartholdi saw the wrong handkerchief and let go of the rope at the wrong moment. Nobody knows for sure. So the rest of this story is mine— as I have imagined it.

Allan Drummond

For Gaye

Special thanks to Geoffrey Dosik, Librarian Technician at the Statue of Liberty and Ellis Island National Monument, and Mary Redmond, Principal Librarian of Public Services at the New York State Library.

Copyright © 2002 by Allan Drummond. All rights reserved
Distributed in Canada by Douglas & McIntyre Ltd.
Color separations by Hong Kong Scanner Arts
Printed and bound in the United States of America by Berryville Graphics
First edition, 2002
1 3 5 7 9 10 8 6 4 2

Library of Congress Cataloging-in-Publication Data
Drummond, Allan.
  Liberty / Allan Drummond.— 1st ed.
    p. cm.
  Summary: Describes the unveiling of the Statue of Liberty and its importance as a symbol of freedom.
  ISBN 0-374-34385-3
  1. Statue of Liberty National Monument (N.Y. and N.J.)—Juvenile fiction. [1. Statue of Liberty
National Monument (N.Y. and N.J.)—Fiction. 2. Freedom—Fiction.] I. Title.

PZ7.D8247 Li 2002
[E]—dc21
                                                                                        2001018777

The day I helped Mr. Bartholdi light up the world,
it rained and rained.

All the umbrellas in the whole city
were out on the streets.

And so were all the flags.

At the waterfront, there was a special ferryboat waiting to carry
Mr. Bartholdi and his friends from France
(and me) . . .

and the harbor was bursting with ships . . .

as we headed out to the island
where they'd built Mr. Bartholdi's statue.

We passed plenty of boats—all sizes—some flying the American flag
and some flying the flag of France.

And all around us people cheered and yelled,
"Liberty!" and "Freedom!"

A big steamship sailed into the harbor from the ocean
loaded with immigrants just arriving from Europe,
coming to America to find liberty and freedom and a better life.

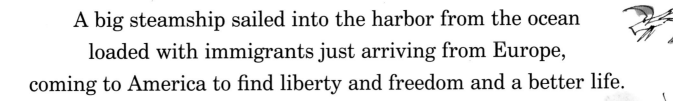

And near the island there was a ferryboat full of women shouting, "How long must *we* wait for liberty?"

It passed very close.

The men who'd put the statue together were there . . .

Constructing a skeleton of iron

On the island stood Mr. Bartholdi's gigantic statue
and crowds and crowds of men.

Building the pedestal

Riveting panels of copper

At work inside Liberty's head

The flame is finished

Installing the spiral stairs inside Liberty

Bartholdi at the workshop in Paris, France, where the statue was made

Shaping Liberty's copper shell

The great lady shows her face

Hand and torch go on display

Liberty first rises above Paris

Le Petit Journal

And the men who'd brought the statue in pieces from France by steamship . . .

And newspapermen and businessmen and engineers, too.

Liberty Enlightening the World,
the Statue of Liberty
—a gift to America from the people of France.

Suddenly Mr. Bartholdi gave me his handkerchief
and asked *me* to help with the signal!

. . . me standing way down below
on the ground,
waiting for a signal from a man in the crowd . . .

and Mr. Bartholdi
way up high,
looking down from Liberty's crown,
waiting for *my* signal
to light up the world!

All those umbrellas . . .

all those flags . . .

and all the ships in the harbor . . .

the smoke and the rain . . .

the man in the crowd waiting . . .

me waiting . . .

Mr. Bartholdi waiting . . .

all the men on the island waiting . . .

the girl and the woman waiting . . .

the President waiting . . .

Then the French girl suddenly sneezed.
I gave her my handkerchief . . .

and suddenly hundreds of white handkerchiefs flashed!
BOOM! a cannon fired. I looked up
and saw that Mr. Bartholdi had already let go of the rope! The flag fell away,
and Lady Liberty's great face was revealed.

Liberty!

Hurrah!

Hooray!

I yelled "Liberty!" as loud as I could.

The French girl cried out *"Liberté!"*

And at sunset Liberty's torch shone out bright
from the land of the free to light up all the world.

Now, the way I see it . . .

I am free . . . and you are free.

We are free . . . We are equal.

We are free . . . to say what we want . . .

and to believe what we want . . .

and we must help others to be free . . .

Freedom is like a flame we must all hold high
and give to others and keep burning bright
all around the world.